For Mom, the Halloween Queen,
and her indoor s'mores
J. H.

For Jaime, Logan, and Bebop
(whom I based some of my pumpkins on)
A. F.

Text copyright © 2014 by Jessie Haas
Illustrations copyright © 2014 by Alison Friend

First edition 2014

Library of Congress Catalog Card Number 2013952844
ISBN 978-0-7636-6450-3

14 15 16 17 18 19 SWT 10 9 8 7 6 5 4 3 2 1

Printed in Dongguan, Guangdong, China

This book was typeset in Dante.
The illustrations were done in gouache.

Candlewick Press
99 Dover Street
Somerville, Massachusetts 02144

visit us at www.candlewick.com

CHAPTER ONE
Fall

Bramble loved fall.

The air was cold and smelled like apples.
It made her feel hungry.

The days were short, but bright and full
of sounds. They made Bramble feel wild
and wide awake.

Honk, honk, honk.
Geese flew across
the sky.
Swish, crinkle, sigh.
An orange leaf
slipped off a tree.

Crunch, crinkle, scritch.

What was that? Bramble turned around, fast. She arched her neck and bugged her eyes out. She trotted around the yard. It was fun pretending to be scared, even if the noise was just her hen, scratching in the leaf pile.

When Maggie came home from school,
she put on Bramble's saddle and bridle. She
got on Bramble's back, and they started
down the street.

Mr. Dingle was working in his yard.
"Be careful," he told Maggie. "That horse
was jumpy today. She acted like she
was afraid of everything."

They went on. Bramble held her head high. She had a bounce in her step. Whenever something moved, she leaped sideways.

A bike!

A dog!

Each time Bramble leaped, Maggie grabbed her mane. She was afraid she might fall off. What did her big horse book say about times like this? Maggie couldn't remember.

A leaf whispered behind them. "Yikes!" Maggie said. "Now you've made *me* jumpy, Bramble. Let's go home."

They were almost there when Bramble froze.

A stranger stood in Mr. Dingle's front yard.

He didn't move. He didn't speak.

Bramble snorted. She stamped her foot.

This time she wasn't pretending.

"That's Mr. Dingle's scarecrow," Maggie
said. "He puts it up every fall. Let's go look
at it." She squeezed Bramble with her legs.
Bramble didn't move.

"It is supposed to scare *birds,* Bramble,"

Maggie said. "You are not a bird!"

No, Bramble was a horse. A smart horse.

Too smart to walk up to this stranger.

Maggie got off. "Mr. Dingle," she called, "may I bring Bramble in to see your scarecrow?"

"Sure," said Mr. Dingle.

Bramble didn't want to go closer. The stranger was *strange*. Why didn't he say something? Why didn't he move?

Maggie led Bramble toward the stranger.
But was that safe? Bramble gave the
stranger a look. If he tried anything, she
would knock him down.

Soon Bramble could see. The stranger was not a person. The face was a broom. The clothes were old clothes, stuffed with hay.

Hay that smelled good.

Hay that *tasted* good.

"Ahem!" said Mr. Dingle. "Please don't eat my scarecrow, Bramble."

CHAPTER TWO
A Fall

The next day was crunchy and cold. Wind whooshed.

The weather made Bramble feel spooky. It made her feel frisky and full of fun. She couldn't wait to go out with Maggie. What would they see today?

People had new things in their yards.

Strange things. Spooky things.

"That is a witch, Bramble." Maggie said.

"Those are pumpkins."

"That is a bag of leaves that is supposed
to look like a pumpkin."

Scritch, crinkle, scritch. Bramble leaped

sideways. What was following them?

"It's just a squirrel," Maggie said. "Don't

be scared, Bramble."

Bramble was only pretending to be scared. She was enjoying herself.

Not Maggie. It was hard to stay in the saddle with Bramble having so much fun.

"I'm not a good enough rider for a day like this," Maggie said. "Let's go home, Bramble."

Just then, a big sound came
from behind them. *KA-PING!*

Bramble turned, very fast.

It was an acorn, bouncing off a roof.

Now Bramble heard another sound.

Thud!

Maggie landed on the
ground beside her.

That was *not* supposed
to happen! Bramble put
her head down. She sniffed
Maggie's face.

"I'm okay," Maggie said.
"Ow! I'm mostly okay."

Maggie knew what her big horse book
said: *If you fall off a horse, get right back on,
before you have time to get scared.*

Too late. Maggie was already scared.

Bramble sniffed Maggie. Why didn't she
get back on?

"I know you're sorry, Bramble," Maggie
said. Her voice shook. "Maybe I will lead
you home. I'll get back on tomorrow."

Bramble didn't move. Sometimes riders fell off in a lesson. They got back on again. Sometimes they didn't want to. But the riders *always* got back on. That made them feel much better.

Bramble stood very still. She made her eyes soft and gentle. She waited.

"I have to, don't I?" Maggie said. "I hope you're saying you'll be good."

She climbed back into the saddle.

Maggie felt high in the air. She held

on tight. Bramble stood still, waiting.

Maggie squeezed with her legs.

"Bramble, walk," she whispered.

Bramble didn't move.

"Bramble, walk," Maggie said.

Bramble turned her head. She looked

up at Maggie.

"I'm okay," Maggie said. "See?" She sat

deeper in the saddle. She put her heels

down. *"Now* will you walk?"

Bramble took one slow step, then another.

Bam, went something behind them.

Maggie jumped. She grabbed Bramble's mane.

Bramble kept walking. Her ears didn't even twitch.

A dog barked—*rarf!* A car horn blew—
bee-ee-p. A neighbor raked leaves—*swish,*
crunch, crinkle!

Bramble ignored the sounds. She was
busy now. She was taking care of Maggie.

CHAPTER THREE

Trick or Treat

"Halloween is coming," Maggie told

Bramble. "Will we be pretty or scary?"

Maggie put on her princess dress. Pretty.

But what would Bramble wear?

Maggie found some curtains and a frilly

scarf. She tried them on Bramble. The scarf

looked very skinny. The curtains sagged.

Maggie said, "Let's be scary instead.

I'll be a headless horseman, Bramble.

You can be the horse."

Maggie went inside. A few minutes

later, a stranger came out of the house.

It staggered toward Bramble.

Bramble backed up.

"It's okay, Bramble," said Maggie's

voice. But where *was* Maggie? Bramble

didn't see her anywhere.

Bramble trotted around. She arched her neck. She bugged her eyes out. She wasn't pretending. She was scared. What was that thing? What had it done to Maggie?

Maggie poked her head out. "Our costume is supposed to scare other people," she said. "It's not supposed to scare you, Bramble."

Mr. Dingle was watching. "I might have an idea," he said.

On Halloween, Bramble was a scarecrow.

Not just any scarecrow — she was Mr.

Dingle's scarecrow.

Maggie was a crow. Dad was Mr. Dingle.

The real Mr. Dingle waved. "Have fun!

I hope Halloween isn't too scary for

Bramble."

Uh-oh! Maggie thought. *I didn't think of that.*

It was getting dark. Strange shapes ran here and there. Maggie held tight to Bramble's mane. "There's nothing to be scared of, Bramble," she said in a shaky voice.

Bramble didn't believe her.

"That's just the witch, Bramble," Maggie
said. "Remember? It's okay." But was it
okay? Or would Bramble do one of
those leaps?

Bramble could tell that Maggie was afraid.
She should get them out of there fast.

But what if Maggie fell off again?

That was NOT going to happen! Bramble
gave the witch a look. If it tried anything, it
would be sorry.

Dad rang a neighbor's doorbell.

"Trick or treat!" Maggie said.

"Oh, good," said the lady at the door.

"I was hoping you'd bring your horse!"

The lady gave Maggie three marshmallow witches. Maggie ate one. She put two in her bag.

She gave Bramble a big crisp apple. That was a surprise! A good surprise.

They went to the next house.

"That's just a jack-o'-lantern, Bramble,"
Maggie said. "Don't be scared."

What jack-o'-lantern? All Bramble saw
was the front door. She marched up to it.
"Wait for me!" Dad said.

Bramble got a carrot. Maggie got peanut-butter cups. At the next house, they got gumdrops. The next neighbor gave them animal crackers.

"Save some for later," Dad said. Maggie did. Bramble didn't. She was doing all the work. She needed to keep up her strength.

Just then, a white shape swooshed
toward them.

Bramble froze. She bugged her eyes out.
Maggie froze, too. She was too surprised
even to hold on.

"BOOOOO!"
a voice said.

Now Bramble could tell. It was just a
kid under a white sheet. The kid had
a bag. Bramble pushed her nose inside.
Peppermints, pretzels—

"Hey!" the kid said. "Stop that!"

He ran away.

Maggie hugged Bramble's neck. "You scared away a ghost, Bramble! You're the bravest horse in the world!" she said.

The last house was Mr. Dingle's. Bramble

rang the bell herself.

"Was Bramble scared?" Mr. Dingle asked.

"Nothing scares Bramble," Maggie said

proudly.

Bramble poked Mr. Dingle. She knew

what was supposed to happen.

Mr. Dingle handed Maggie a basket

of corn.

Some of it was real corn. Some of it was candy corn. "Save some for the hen," he said.

Bramble ate some candy corn. She ate some real corn. She was starting to feel full.

Back home, Maggie took off their
costumes. She gave Bramble some hay.

Bramble turned her back. She would
save the hay for later.

"Too full?" Maggie said. "I know how
you feel."